BESTIES

WORK IT OUT

BESTIES
WORK IT OUT

BY KAYLA MILLER & JEFFREY CANINO
ART BY KRISTINA LUU

ETCH
HOUGHTON MIFFLIN HARCOURT
BOSTON   NEW YORK

Color by Damali Beatty
Lettering by Lauren Prescott
Illustrations & additional color by Kristina Luu

Based on the Click series, created by Kayla Miller

Etch is an imprint of Houghton Mifflin Harcourt Publishing Company.

hmhbooks.com

The illustrations in this book were done in Clip Studio Paint with digital brushes.
Cover and interior design by Andrea Miller and Stephanie Hays

ISBN 978-0-358-52115-0 hardcover
ISBN 978-0-358-56191-0 softcover
ISBN 978-0-358-61155-4 signed edition

Manufactured In China
SCP 10 9 8 7 6 5 4 3 2 1
4500824226

For every bestie I've made
along the way. —K.M.

For Mom. —J.C.

For Molly & Milo, my
four-legged besties. —K.L.

3

So, what sort of fabulous concoction is "Rainbowade"?

TRY OUR RAINBOWADE 75¢

Only the latest craze in fruit juice technology.

Everybody will be talking about it.

We thought: Aren't we all **over** pink and yellow lemonade?

So last season.

Nothing against the colors pink and yellow—

I love pink, **personally.**

—but we think consumers are ready for refreshment that will match any mood or outfit...

...all while keeping that same classic taste.

Patent pending.

Aren't **we** supposed to pick the colors?

Oops.

Uh...did we pick wrong?

Actually, these **are** our favorite colors. You pair have got talent. What do we owe you?

We'll look for your ads on TV!

Thanks for the drinks, girls!

That went well... but next time, let's remember to let the customers **order** before we make them anything!

Look! And that's plus the $1.50 they paid for the drinks!

We'll be rich by suppertime!

Hey, Ivan! You thirsty?

Whoa. I was just thinking about how thirsty I was.

How'd **you** know that?

Pick a color, any color, and we'll quench your thirst with our magical Rainbowade!

Black, please.

Uh, sure...

Yum!

Seventy-five cents, please.

Huh? Oh, sorry—

I didn't know it cost money.

Just take it.

It's fine. Feel that sun. We'll be swimming in coins soon.

Let's try to look on the bright side...

How can we?

Life's giving us lemons when we already **made** the lemonade.

8

10

Don't stay up too late, Chanda!

Brilliant young minds need at least 9.5 hours of sleep, even if it **is** the weekend.

If we subtract the cost of the lemons, sugar, food coloring, cups, paper straws, and dog treats, that leaves us with...

...zero dollars, zero cents, and a fridge full of lemonade.

PLOOMF!

I guess I have to forget about buying my mom that gift certificate to the spa for her birthday...

PLOOMPH!

At this rate, I'll be lucky if I can afford to buy her a sheet mask and a scented candle from the dollar store.

I'm sorry, Beth. I thought we'd be able to solve your money problem today.

I just really wanted to do something nice for her.

She does so much for my whole family.

And now I can't even help to give her one special day off.

Don't think like that. We'll get you the money.

Really? How?

I haven't figured out that part yet. But if we set our minds to it, I'm sure we'll think of something...

After all, it's **us** doing the thinking.

Worst comes to worst, we'll dig under every couch cushion

and recycle every soda can that we have to.

I guess today didn't go exactly how **you** planned, either.

What do you mean? I totally **love** when my parents fail to notice my accomplishments.

SUNDAY MORNING.

Whatcha doin'?

Checking the animal shelter's website.

There was an open adoption event yesterday, and I wanted to see who got adopted.

Any kittens left?

What's the use? If I can't prove to my parents that I'm responsible enough to take care of a pet, then it's hopeless.

FWIP

Whenever I bring it up, my dad says, "Maybe when you're older, chickoo."

I'll be wrinkled and gray by the time I'm "old enough."

Maybe we need to give them another example of how mature you are.

??

Like how?

GRUMBLE GRUMBLE

Like **breakfast!**

17

18

19

GRRRRRRRRRRRRRRRRrrrrrr

Maybe you can try again when I'm not around.

I might as well make them *macaroni necklaces* next time...

That's the most they'd expect from me.

20

Hey, Dad. Hi, Johnny.

Hi, girls.

'Sup, Beth. Hey, Chanda.

Hi, Mom.

Can we help you out?

No, sweetheart, I'm fine.

Just about to wrap up.

But take a cupcake before John's teammates make them disappear.

Your mom **deserves** that spa day.

Uh-huh!

Hey, pip-squeaks. How'd the lemonade stand go?

Rainbowade, Lisa. And it went awful.

Also maybe cool it with the "pip-squeaks." It's a sore spot at the moment.

No, Beth, Lisa's right. We're pip-squeaks. Pip-squeaks with nothing but lemonade and a shattered dream.

Tell me all about it, my big squeaks.

I'm sorry it didn't go well. I don't think that you should be too discouraged.

Lemonade stands are **rarely** where the big bucks are.

Mom's birthday is more than a week away, Beth. And even if you can't scrounge up the dough, she'll love whatever you're able to do for her.

And, Chanda, adopting a cat would obviously complete your vibe. I'm confident your parents will see that eventually.

I'm sorry I can't stay and eat cupcakes with you both until we all feel better, but lacrosse practice calls.

BZZT ♪
BZZT ♫

M. Langford

Looks like Ms. Langford also calls.

Who's that?

An old lady who lives down the street. Lisa dog-sits for her sometimes.

Hi, Ms. Langford! How are you today?

For the next week? I'm sorry, Ms. Langford. I'd love to help you out, but with my practice schedule and my art show coming up...

Hey, wait a second...

What if I told you I could get you **two** mature and responsible dog-sitting professionals for the price of one?

Good news, squeaks.

fortune—and Ms. Langford—shines favorably upon you.

She wants you both to go over to her place after school tomorrow.

Unless you make a major goof in the first five minutes, you've got the job.

Yeah, yeah, you can thank me later!

And you will— Ms. Langford's is a sweet gig.

You've still got the directions to Ms. Langford's that Lisa made us?

All safe and stylish.

28

Wow.

What a relief.

Anybody with baby Bambis around her yard probably doesn't toss kids into her oven.

C'mon, Beth.

RIIING

Game faces?

To summarize, your duties are watering the plants and the garden, bringing in the mail, and making sure Baxter has food, water, and his walksies two times a day.

He has a doggy door into the yard so he can take care of his business when you're not here, but Baxter simply *loves* his walksies.

It couldn't be simpler.

Is that...

...A WALK-IN CLOSET!?

I bet if we were this rich and famous, we wouldn't have to ask our parents' permission for anything.

With the money this all cost, Ms. Langford could buy herself a spa *year*!

Chanda, we'd have to turn to a life of crime to afford this kind of luxury.

I'll tell you what I think...

I think it would be a crime **not** to try this on!

37

39

Looking smart, Chanda.

Smashing, Beth.

Hey! Follow me...

Look! I noticed this fainting couch earlier. Isn't it dramatic?

The perfect place to collapse when Baxter tires us out.

Oh, no, darling.

I couldn't possibly walk another runway.

Hold that pose. I need to grab my camera.

These are primo pics for our followers.

OooF!

It's getting kind of late. I guess we better put everything back where we found it.

I want to be home in time to help my mom with dinner.

Beth Wagner: Daughter Extraordinaire.

It's not that... It's just that spending all afternoon pretending to live like divas...

...has me thinking about my parents and how all they do is work.

The last nice thing they did for themselves was go out for dinner together to Professor Pizza's Parlor the one night they both had off.

And that was **months ago.**

So I feel like anything I can do to help out my mom and dad is worth it.

Even if it's just microwaving frozen veggies.

crystalchandalier:
Flowers: growing.
Beth: glowing.
#garden #vintagefashion
#adorbs
frantastic09:
ooooOOOOooooooooo!!
willowXtheXwisp: This
is SO good <3 <3

⭐ 73   💬 6   ⬆️

crystalchandalier:
Teatime all the time.
#scrumptious #scrump
#pinkiesup
trentsk8s808: save
some cookies for
meeeeeeee!!!!!
graaaceful: classy and
classic

⭐ 70   💬 10   ⬆️

crystalchandalier: Which one of you has been shedding on the couch? **@b3thw** #baddog #badbaxter #badbeth
avacheers4u: I hope that's faux
crystalchandalier: @avacheers4u Beth's is acrylic, Baxter's is homegrown

⭐ 83 💬 19 ⬆️

crystalchandalier: It's not New Year's, but we're still having a ball! #besties #bestdog #clink
livitup1016: lol i always cheers with orange juice too #nopulp
naturalbornchiller: OMG where are you???

⭐ 76 💬 12 ⬆️

You'll find out tomorrow when **you** have the morning shift...

Not that...

Our fashion shoot!

Those fave counts are in the top tier of the sixth grade, Beth. I've checked.

And I don't want to freak you out... but even some **seventh graders** faved them.

Seventy of our classmates agree that I'm glowing.

I didn't think that many knew who I was!

51

No red carpet, but that's understandable.

We didn't give them a whole lot of time to prepare.

I don't know... What if people faved them as a goof?

Some of the pictures were pretty silly.

Silly is **in** right now. Funny videos are all anybody talks about during lunch lately.

Plus, nobody can deny that we made silly look chic.

People might talk about **us** during lunch.

Chanda! Beth! Over here!

Hey, guys.

Hi!

We were just talking about the fun photos you posted.

They were so great! Those outfits!

Trent and I are big fans of Baxter. Comedy legend.

I'd like to shake his paw.

Where is that place, anyway? I've been to enough birthday parties to know that's not either of your houses.

Beth and I are dog-sitting for a woman who lives down the street from us.

We think she must be a retired Hollywood actor. She has the coolest décor and a walk-in closet a mile deep.

That explains its showbiz charm!

So can we expect more snapshots from the glamorous lives of Beth and Chanda?

Count on it.

Tell Baxter "good boy" for us.

Beth, Chanda, you have **got** to spill about that peachy pad where you were staying.

Has this town been hiding some quaint bed-and-breakfast that no one's told me about?

Oh, that place? It's Ms. Langford's house.

She's an old family friend. Asks us to look after her things when she's out of town.

It's basically a second home to Beth and me.

Why'd you say that back there about Ms. Langford?

What did I say?

That we're old friends and always hang out at her place.

She hardly knows us.

That's true now.

But I'm sure we'll be good friends by the time she gets back and sees what a great job we did.

Also, this overnight popularity thing feels like a sugar rush.

I think I'm just spouting out whatever makes us sound coolest.

Hey, guys, wait up!

So, you're inviting me over, right?

Uh...

Huh?

I **have** to see your place.

It reminds me so much of this boutique hotel where my mom and I stayed in France.

Well, I guess maybe that's something we could do...

It **is** practically your own home, right?

Is there a problem?

No! No problem— of course not.

Okaaaay. Let me know, will you?

I don't know, Chanda...

I've already been feeling bad that we went through all of Ms. Langford's stuff without permission.

Inviting Nat over to visit seems extra bad.

Remember what Ms. Langford said before she left?

"Make yourselves feel at home." That sounds like permission to me.

When I'm home, I try on tons of outfits and invite over my friends.

I don't think she meant it **literally**.

And even if she did, taking this job is supposed to be about us showing that we're mature and we take our responsibilities seriously.

Inviting a friend over to drink tea and admire interior design sounds super mature to me!

Listen, just because everyone thinks we're cool now doesn't mean they will tomorrow.

Nat, on the other hand, is cool and popular every day.

And she wants to hang out with us...

At least **today** she does. She never has before! Think about it, Beth. Being responsible and popular could be a serious makeover for us.

Did you hear that Nat's dad took her and Ava

to an art museum in the city last weekend?

Of course—everyone has! And the week before that,

she threw a slumber party for all the cheerleaders to show off her new karaoke machine.

Okay, we're inviting her over.

Wagner! You're up.

Home run!

61

Nat!

Hey, Chanda. What's up?

Beth and I talked it over, and we agree that you should definitely come by the house after school.

Ah, I was wondering whose phone number that was.

I texted you the address.

Meet us there at 4:00?

Wouldn't miss it.

3:00 P.M.

PHEW

PLO OMFF!

Invite delivered.

We've got one hour to run through all the chores, get ready, and make sure Baxter's all set.

YIP!

YAP!

I'm worried Baxter doesn't understand houseguests...

63

If it's anything like this morning, prepare for him to pounce at us...

...or not.

She's here!

UH...

THEY'RE HERE?

Welcome to our pad! Please, come inside.

This is the front room!

Here you'll find trinkets, houseplants, and tasteful wall art.

I love it.

Your friend has such cool stuff.

This place looked bigger in the pictures.

Wait until you see the open floor design of the main room. Living room, kitchen, and dining room all in one!

An antique dealer's paradise!

Oh no! That's awful.

Is there anything we can do to help?

No! No, it's fine. Ms. Langford will understand. She's cool about little accidents.

How could she not be with Baxter as her roommate?

Point me in the direction of a broom and I'll get to work.

Thanks, Ava. But no, we're good.

It's just one of those things...

No you don't—get up.

We're fine. We can fix this.

How? What can we do? It's in pieces...

Yeah, but these are clean breaks.

Totally fixable.

Especially...

...when we have...

...the right tool!

SPARKLE GLUE

78

Chanda, that's glitter glue! This isn't a glitter lamp!

Remember when we used this to spruce up our electron diagram in science class? It dried with only half the dazzle we expected.

And to think we almost threw the rest out!

Perfect! You can't even tell.

You can tell.

That's what it always looked like!

Oh yeah, how could I forget it was bleeding glitter before we wrecked it!

Okay, that's not fair. We didn't exactly knock it over ourselves.

Chanda! We weren't supposed to have people over! It's our fault.

They won't be mad. They'll never have to know. We can still figure this out.

But how?

I don't think glitter glue is going to help us now.

No, but this might: Look! The artist signed her name on the bottom of the lamp.

I had a feeling this wasn't some department-store piece.

So maybe, just maybe, if we search for her on the Internet...

Oooooh!

Here we go.

You'd think for that much money it would at least be indestructible.

The worst part is that the replacement probably costs more than whatever Ms. Langford is going to pay us for this entire week of Baxter Duty.

I think you mean "more than she **was** going to pay us."

We can still make things right, Beth.

I hope so. Because this feels all **wrong**.

No way.

But Amaya is old and responsible and has a job. She definitely has the money to loan us.

Amaya still treats me like a silly little kid.

There's no way she'd give us the money without ratting us out to my parents, and if that happens, I won't be allowed to even look at a cat until I'm 30.

Okay, but we can't ask Lisa, either.

Why not? We can actually trust her. She never tells on us for **anything**.

Remember how she took the blame for the time we spilled nail polish all over the carpet? We didn't even ask her to do that.

Exactly. Lisa does too much for us already. She might have the money, but she's been saving up so she can frame her paintings for that big art show.

It wouldn't be right to ask her for money when she needs it herself.

If we can't ask either of our sisters, I don't think there's anyone we **can** ask.

That's fair. It's our mess.

Maybe we turn ourselves in and beg for mercy.

Does that sound like us? We've got until next Monday —that's six days!— before Ms. Langford comes home.

Okay, then what's another option?

All we have to do is solve for x!

$$(B+C) + X = \$\$\$$$

WEDNESDAY MORNING.
FIVE DAYS UNTIL DOOMSDAY.

I'm starting to worry...

I keep checking, but we haven't gotten any emails yet.

Relax. We papered the town with ads. People will definitely notice.

It's just still early. I'm sure our first customers are typing us messages over their morning coffee as we speak.

But what if someone else buys the lamp while we're waiting?

What if nobody hires us and we never make the money we need?

I smell lemons.

Do you smell lemons?

That's the scent of failure, Beth! Snap out of it!

91

LUNCHTIME.

Usually when I see the "New Message" icon I get butterflies in my stomach. Right now I feel like I could kiss the screen!

If we add Olive's, that's four gigs lined up before we've finished our yogurts. And all totally doable this week, if we manage our time right.

We're learning an important lesson, Beth: Never underestimate how badly people don't want to do their chores.

Hey, girls. My mom saw your flyer.

She asked me if you know how to get rid of the busted vintage motorcycle in the garage she's been bugging my dad about.

Uh, that's not our specialty...

Are you sure **you** don't want to help him out?

Pfft. Yeah, right. He wouldn't pay **me**.

Yeah, that's what I told her. In that case, she said my dad could use some help repainting his home office.

93

We're **lucky** to have this much work already lined up for our first day as professional multitaskers.

At this rate, we might actually make the money we need in time.

Bee-tee-dub, tomorrow and Friday are filling up too. A couple more emails came in while you and Baxter were out.

We're going to have to start turning customers away if this keeps up.

That's the power of a well-designed flyer. Oh yeah, speaking of, I gave one to Mr. Florez's husband at the dog park. He's got something for us.

More dog walking?

Can you believe nobody wants to walk their dog in this heat?

Rainbowade... Today could have been your day...

WEDNESDAY, 3:42 P.M.

WEDNESDAY, 4:38 P.M.

Can I change my mind and take the big ones?

YIP YIP

WEDNESDAY, 5:13 P.M.

I want to thank you two again for helping out Olive and me.

All of my staff begged off this week. I'm guessing to hit the beach.

Without you, sorting these donated books for the sale would have kept us busy until next Tuesday.

And the sale's this weekend! So you guys are pretty much superheroes.

WEDNESDAY, 6:30 P.M.

How was your day, girls?

Busy.

THURSDAY, 3:15 P.M.
FOUR DAYS UNTIL DOOMSDAY.

THURSDAY, 4:45 P.M.

THURSDAY, 5:37 P.M.

THURSDAY, 7:47 P.M.

I know we should put it away in case your parents walk in.

But maybe we can look at it for just another minute.

99

This is why I didn't want to put "Entertainment" on the flyer!

You know what the stakes are.

Plus, what have we been practicing for, if not for a moment like this?

Ready, girls?

Everything's set. I'll be the deejay.

ZIP ZIP

100

Nailed it.

Girls, I don't know if you realize it, but you just made me Grandma of the Year.

After Whizzo the Space Clown had to cancel at the last minute, my Clara's heart was broken.

But you two showed her that astronauts don't just have to walk on the moon.

They can also *moonwalk*.

You'll find I threw in more than we agreed upon. You earned it.

Did we make it?

I don't know if there are any dogs left for us to walk in the entire neighborhood.

Did we ever!

I was worried we wouldn't have enough left over for the next-day shipping, but this covers it.

I've been messaging the new lamp's seller on StuffSwap.

I explained to her how quickly we need it to arrive, and she said she can have it shipped out first thing tomorrow, as long as we send her the money by tonight.

Hooray! Doomsday deflected! This calls for celebratory facials and binge-watching!

I don't see anything stopping us from rewatching the last two seasons of Larkspur Academy this weekend.

Except for Monday's homework.

UGH!

My darling sister, Lisa.

My bestie's darling sister, Lisa.

SLAM!

Whatever it is: no thank you.

107

TEN MINUTES LATER...

You guys... You really **blew it.**

We know. Ms. Langford's place is so cool...

We got carried away wanting to show it off.

We're sorry we let you down.

I just don't understand why you'd think any of what you did was okay.

You shouldn't dig through other people's things, and you definitely shouldn't invite people over to a house that doesn't belong to you. This is Responsible Employed Teenager 101 stuff.

Trust me. When you get to be my age, what makes you cool isn't how many faves you have on social media.

It's whether or not you can afford a car. So, it's wise not to mess up your income sources.

How many dogs would we have to walk to buy a car?

A hundred?

Oh, the sweet innocence of youth.

Well, you're lucky that my recommending you makes me feel partially responsible for the broken lamp.

Bring me my laptop and let's order the thing.

I can't believe **this** is my first-ever online purchase with my first-ever debit card.

We'll make it up to you somehow.

You bet you will.

But, y'know, I have to say I'm impressed by the hustle.

I've never made this much money in a week. Granted, I haven't **lost** this much in a week either.

Could be worse. At least now Langford will pay you.

You've also cleverly avoided being grounded by coming to me instead of Mom and Dad,

so you'll still have the chance to find some more odd jobs out in the great, wide world if you want.

Anyway, the lamp is ordered. You can leave the money on my desk.

I've gotta go help Dad with dinner or else it's definitely going to be another Pizza Bagel Friday.

But, Lisa...

Pizza Bagel Friday is a **tradition**.

We love you, Lisa.

And we'll never goof up like that again.

Let's not make promises we can't keep.

I mean, we might goof up in a **new** way...

Hi, everyone. Don't you all look cozy.

Hi, Mom!

You fed them, right?

They're not going to turn feral on me?

Oh, I'm sure the bread and cheese they're stuffed with will slow them down.

I hope everyone isn't too full.

Johnny, be a dear and bring inside what's on the passenger seat.

Sure thing, Mom.

You'll have to catch me up on the movie.

What's Johnny getting from the car, Mom?

MILK SHAKES!

Somehow, I knew to have them make one extra.

You're the **best**, Mrs. Wagner.

Behold! The perks of success!

Also known as some snacks your mom packed us.

I didn't have the heart to tell her we're not on speaking terms with lemonade.

Drinking terms, however...

You look stressed, Beth. What's wrong?

I don't know... It just seems like everything is starting to go right,

so I'm worried that we're due for another **something bad** to happen.

Cat on the brain again?

Only **always.** I've got a massive wish list of essential items saved on Kitten Warehouse.

Adoptions from the shelter are free, so I'll be able to spoil my future kitty with as many toys and treats as I can afford.

Speaking of, I wonder how much Ms. Langford is going to pay us.

I'm not sure... But Lisa says she pays well.

SUNDAY MORNING.

We thought we'd return the favor this weekend, girls.

You know, Dad, the shelter is having another adoption event next week. Spring is an important time to adopt because the shelters have a lot of stray kittens arriving off the streets.

We'll see, chickoo.

Don't you still have another animal under your care at the moment?

Yeah—we're heading over to walk Baxter after we finish eating.

Ms. Langford comes back home tomorrow after school.

So I suppose real soon I'm going to have a lot of time to devote to the care and protection of other fluffy friends.

It's excellent timing.

Convenient indeed.

How is little Baxter?

From what Chanda tells us, he seems a handful.

When we left him yesterday, he'd tired himself out and was sleeping like an angel...

...which means now he's probably running up the walls waiting for us.

AHAHAHAHAHAHAHAHAHAHAHAHA

SUNDAY, NOON.

Okay, the tracking app says the package should be here sometime between 12:00 and 2:00.

We can finish our homework by the window so we can see the truck when it pulls up.

Any change?

Still "Out for Delivery."

I'll keep refreshing, though.

What's the matter?

This is the same lamp, right?

It's **def** the lamp. Hmmm.

SCREE

Then why are you still frowning?

Something looks **off**...

!!!

UGHHHHHHHH

129

131

Fabric section is over there. I think that's where you'll find the trim.

I'll be in the back at the framing department, if you need me.

See anything?

No.

These all look really different.

Wait, I think I see some beaded trim...

How about this one?

It's the right color... The pattern is a bit different, but it's close.

135

I'm sorry, no. Store policy.

If you can't afford the roll, I'll put it back for you.

Chanda...

I'm fine.

I'm just frustrated.

We're so close to being able to fix everything...

138

140

MONDAY MORNING. DOOMSDAY.

That's the last of them.

I'm gonna head into school early to get these unloaded. Want a ride over to Ms. Langford's?

Yeah, that would be nice. Let me grab my bag.

And the lamp.

Anything on your mind, squeak?

No, I'm okay. Just tired.

I didn't sleep well.

I couldn't help but notice that you and Chanda didn't speak the whole ride home yesterday.

If something happened, you know you can talk to me about it.

I hope you guys didn't get into a fight about me offering to buy the trim.

I would have been happy to help you out.

I know. It's not that. It's just... It's not your problem, Lisa. None of this is.

I've got to take responsibility.

You might play sweet when others are around, but I know your true morning self, widdle Baxter...

Baxter?

Oh...

Hi, Chanda. I thought it was my morning with Baxter.

You walked him last night.

Fair's fair.

Oh, right.

I guess so...

You brought the lamp?

Yeah—it's at the front door.

I missed you on the bus today.

My mom drove me.

SLAM!

See you in class, then...

Hey, Beth. Where's your equally-as-good half?

She's sitting over with Ava and the other cheerleaders.

Beth without Chanda? That's like...

...cheese without crackers!

Cookies without milk!

Sure, they're still great on their own, but together is even better.

I don't think Chanda feels that way at the moment.

We got into a fight yesterday...

I'm sorry, Beth. I've been there. It's never a fun feeling.

What happened?

So much.

But I lost my temper and said some things I probably shouldn't have.

I want to apologize, but she's not making it easy...

She might not be ready to hear it yet.

I'm sure she will be eventually.

And then we feel better.

Yeah— works every time!

Every friendship is different.

I'll walk Baxter. You can do the house chores.

We'll set up the lamp when I get back.

Let's get this over with.

Chanda...

Chanda, I want to talk.

COUGH.

I got upset because you said what I was doing was **selfish**.

But I haven't been doing any of this for me. I don't care if I'm grounded for the rest of the year...

...except for what it would mean for **her**.

COUNTESS PAWSBURY

AGE: 11
BREED: PERSIAN

I always thought you wanted a kitten...

When I started learning about how to adopt a cat...

...I read about how older cats are so much less likely to be chosen for adoption because everybody always wants kittens.

I've been following all of the adoptions from this shelter for the past month.

Almost every cat has found a home, but nobody has adopted Countess Pawsbury.

She's been living there for six months, since her owners lost their home and had to give her up.

When I think about her at the shelter all day, watching as all the other cats and kittens get played with and taken away to new homes...

...I just...

Oh, Chanda.

I'm sorry I called you selfish. You're not.

You're a stubborn, selfless *sweetheart*.

The "stubborn" part sounds right.

Adopting the Countess has become so important to me that it's hard to see things from anyone else's point of view.

I'm sorry I didn't tell you about her before now.

I guess I was worried you'd think it was a mistake or that she was too old or ugly...

Are you kidding? I love her already, and we haven't even met yet.

I'm not so sure you'll ever have the pleasure now.

When Ms. Langford gets here and sees that thing, we're toast.

Cheer up, partner. Maybe Ms. Langford won't notice the missing fringe and everything will work out fine.

Maybe she hates this lamp and never even looks at it!

I don't know... I meant what I said before about feeling like a little kid.

Maybe everything that's happened means my parents are right, and I'm really **not** responsible enough to take care of a pet...

I just hope that **someone** will want to adopt the Countess and give her a good home.

You do?!

Of course.

Baxter the Horrible strikes again. You naughty, naughty boy.

Breaking the lamp and scaring the girls like that!

Shame on you.

Sure thing, Ms. Langfo—

No...

No! I meant no, Baxter didn't break your lamp.

I bumped into it when we were trying to settle him down. *I* broke your lamp.

No, you won't sweep up the lamp?

Well, **we** did... That lamp on the ground isn't even yours.

We broke the original last week when we invited some friends over to look at all of your great plants and décor and Baxter got too excited.

Which was totally our fault! We were **irresponsible**.

We shouldn't have had anyone over here for Baxter to get excited about.

And we're so, so, so, so sorry that we took advantage of your trust.

We bought the new lamp to try to make everything **better**...

...but I guess we just made it all **worse**.

We know we don't deserve to be paid for our work this week.

We probably deserve a lot worse for what we've done. But, please...please...

...don't tell our parents. It's not that we're trying to avoid being punished. Punish us!

We'll walk Baxter for free for the rest of the year, if that's what it takes!

But if Chanda's parents find out what we did, they'll never trust her again.

And if they don't trust her, they'll never allow her to adopt that sweet, lonely cat from the shelter that you saw in the video.

We'll do anything if it means we can save Countess Pawsbury.

I don't care how many rooms I have to paint or cars I have to wash or kids' birthday parties I have to sing at—

—I'll earn back all of the money so that you can still give your mom a special spa day!

And you can forget Kitten Warehouse and their ridiculous prices!

I'll **make** Countess Pawsbury a canopy bed.

I can use my dad's tools to build a frame, and we'll use my sewing machine to sew some curtains...

Contrary to what you might believe, you two earned this.

I will, of course, be calling your parents...

...to report how pleased I was to find my Baxter so well cared for this past week.

That is, so long as you promise **not** to invite any of your friends over the next time I ask you to watch the house.

Of course. Thank you, Ms. Langford.

I always thought my parents and teachers were trying to trick me with that whole "honesty is the best policy" business.

Lisa would say it's the **better** policy.

And y'know what's better about being a responsible grownup than what Lisa told us?

What?

The pay.

THE NEXT WEEKEND...

SNAPOGRAPH

POST

Bonjour! After six months of living at the Tri-County Animal Shelter, the Countess is off seeing the world (from the comfort of our bedroom)! Not every elder cat is so fortunate. There are countless cats at shelters waiting to find their forever homes. Do you have room in your life for a furry friend? #adoptdontshop #adoptold #purr #catsofsnapograph

Where's the Countess?

How is she? Still a total darling?

I want Lisa and my mom to meet her!

Shhh—she's resting.

We can play with her for a bit when we get back later.

Cats need **way** more beauty sleep than people do, Beth.

And if the Countess wants to keep her status as a social media superstar, every wink counts.

Has she stopped purring?

Not since we got home from the shelter last Tuesday.

She must be getting sick of it!

Are you sure you two want to spend all of your housesitting money taking Lisa and me to the spa?

It's a very sweet gesture, but I know how hard you two worked for the money.

She must never know.

Read the *New York Times* best-selling series from

Kayla Miller

A Q&A WITH THE BESTIES TEAM

Q: Could everyone speak to what their role in *Besties* is?

KAYLA: I'm one of the authors, and after a lot of planning with Jeffrey, I write the outline for the story and come back at the end of the process to help tighten up the dialogue and jokes.

JEFFREY: As a coauthor, I develop the story with Kayla and then write the full script.

KRISTINA: I am the main illustrator, so I'm inking and drawing—essentially taking the script and bringing it to life.

DAMALI: I'm the colorist, and it's my job to take all the locals and flesh out the scenes that Kristina draws. Locals, or local colors, are the standard hues you would assign to each object.

Q: Kayla, *Besties* reflects an expansion of the world that you've established in *Click*. What did you most respond to about directions that Jeffrey took?

KAYLA: I really liked the humor and energy that Jeffrey brought to the story. We wanted the book to have that feeling of when you're a kid or a tween and you're with your best friend and the crazy antics that you get up to. Like a never-ending sleepover! I also enjoyed how Jeffrey took the characters and developed their voices through the dialogue and expanded their personalities.

Q: What did you most respond to about the direction Kristina took?

KAYLA: How expressive the art is! The facial expressions are big and fun and lively. The attention to detail makes the world of Besties feel really full and lived in.

Q: Jeffrey, were there themes in *Besties* you especially wanted to explore?

JEFFREY: I was most interested in exploring how Beth and Chanda were going to deal with the new concerns in their lives. Money, family, or status can be abstract to younger kids, but when you hit that tween or teenage stage, they become important in your life . . . to the extent that you're concerned with them and your actions start to matter in a new way. Seeing how the girls were going to deal with those new pressures—how they were going to figure out what mattered to them and make the right choices from there—was very fun to explore.

Q: What did you want to bring forward from the Click storytelling?

JEFFREY: The things I like most about Kayla's books are the heart and kindness of them. They're extremely optimistic. They show growth between friends and people. There's not a desire to write people off or give up. So I wanted to bring that here. These girls are not averse to getting into trouble, but there's this core of love that I think is really important.

Q: Jeffrey, can you share some insights into fine-tuning the dialogue?

JEFFREY: It took about half of the first book to figure out what their voices were. There was definitely a lot of going back and revising. It dawned on me that they're kind of like an old comedy duo. They're both funny but in different ways. Beth is more self-effacing. She has a huge heart that I think is her most defining quality, whereas Chanda has somewhat wild schemes that can get them into trouble. They bounce off each other well so that it doesn't seem like they have the same voice, but they have an established dynamic between them.

Q: Kristina, what about **Besties** did you connect with most?

KRISTINA: The thing that touches me about **Besties** and Kayla's books in general is that I can picture myself in my youth or in these exact situations that these girls are in. I feel like I'm channeling the inner twelve-year-old me while I'm working on these books!

Q: How has working on a team been different than working on your webcomic?

KRISTINA: I'm much more used to taking the reins, but in this case there's back and forth. It's nice to have someone to count on to provide another perspective that I haven't considered. For example, how Damali sometimes takes my work in a different direction with colors and it's so much better. I love the cooperative aspect of this because everyone provides the best of what they specialize in, and it becomes something better than what I could have done on my own.

Kristina, inking a page!

Q: Dàmàli, could you describe your collaborative process with Kristina?

DAMALI: The way we've been working so far is that every two weeks I'll get a big batch of pages, somewhere between 16 and 20 pages, and we've come up with a system that breaks down how we do the pages so that it's easiest to edit in a collaborative way. We've made layers, so that if one of us needs to correct a color on a character, it's really easy to pinpoint where that problem area is and correct it. I typically do all the flats at once, which is when you put down the colors of each object, then I come back later on and do things like shading, rounding things out, and tweaking color details, like adding sparkles.

Q: Dàmàli, can you speak to ways you and Kristina use color to add to the story?

DAMALI: Color is a really big part of the story. I think a lot in color. I think that the color of ***Besties*** speaks to the vibe that we're giving off in the story. It's very much, you're a tween, it's you and your best friend. Every day your whole world is so lush and full of so many possibilities. I really get that when I read through the story. It reminds me of my own childhood and my own bestie! So the way that we play with color, the way that we make everything bright, the way that we make things pop—especially when it comes to outdoor spaces, Ms. Langford's house, the outfits that the girls get to wear—it's all a reflection of the vibrancy and the excitement with which they approach their world, just like their relationships.

Q: Do you have a favorite scene in the book?

KAYLA: I have two favorite scenes. I really like the second lamp break where Baxter is running in circles around the room and jumping on everything. I haven't had a lot of chances with the Click books to write physical comedy, so it was fun figuring out each thing that needed to happen for that lamp to smash. That was the only scene Jeffrey and I wrote together, and it involved me running around the house and showing how Baxter would do this, and then Beth would lean like that, so it was just a really fun experience of writing that scene. As far as my favorite scene in the finished book . . . I really like the dressing up in Ms. Langford's closet scene. It reminds me of all the dressing room montages in movies from the 1990s and early 2000s. It's just so fun and brings me back to my childhood.

JEFFREY: My favorite scene is their final odd job being entertainers at the birthday party. I enjoyed writing the song, for one. The costumes— everything about it was a joy to squeeze in there at the end.

KRISTINA: My favorite scene is actually one of the sadder parts of the book, when the girls are fighting and they go to school. There's something about that part that really got me like, wow, I know exactly what this feeling is, because we've all been there. We've all had a fight with our sibling, or our best friend at school, or one of our classmates. And you feel that almost-physical woe, especially when you're young. It becomes so tangible. You guys did a really good job of writing that down, so making that part in the book was super fun, but also touching in a way. I'm having fun the whole time, so it was just kind of a switch when I got to this part. It was like, *whoa!*

DAMALI: I like the scenes with Lisa in them. I'm also an older sister and I find her relatable. After the girls confess about what happened at Ms. Langford's house and she was like, "OK, you can't do that. You can't break people's stuff and you can't wear their clothes when they're not around"—that was my thought when I saw that dress-up montage. *That's fun, but those aren't your clothes!*

Q: Do you have something you're hoping readers will take away from the book?

KAYLA: I always come back to how I want my readers to communicate with other people. So many of the problems that we face are misunderstandings that come about because we're not expressing ourselves clearly. So I think sharing your problems with others, talking with other people, and communicating clearly could help a lot of situations.

JEFFREY: I want to add on to what Kayla said, because that's true even in a best friend relationship. This book is very much about how you need to nourish that relationship. We can fall into thinking that your best friend is your best friend—you don't necessarily need to worry about them, they're always going to be there— but that might not be the case, especially if you don't make the effort to figure out where your best friend is at. There are these little moments of miscommunication or omitted communication between Beth and Chanda that they learn to work through. It makes their friendship stronger.

KRISTINA: I think the main lesson is that, overall, friendship takes work, and just because something gets bad doesn't mean it's always going to stay bad. The most wonderful relationships and friendships you have may face big conflict or have some problems that aren't always easy to navigate. But working through it is so worth it. Even when things feel really tough or uncomfortable, making the effort to figure things out can only make your friendships stronger.

A PAGE FROM START TO FINISH

A look at the first thumbnails from the authors

Then over to Kristina!

Sketches

Inks

finished color

Or as Beth and Chanda would say:

VOILÀ!

DESIGNING BETH & CHANDA

Kristina's initial drawings. She upped the stylish duo's fashion game as she developed the characters.

CHANDA BASU

BETH WAGNER

Kristina's initial character
lineup of Beth and her family

Kristina's initial character lineup of
Chanda, her family, Ms. Langford, and Baxter

ACKNOWLEDGMENTS

We would like to thank everyone at HMH for giving us the opportunity to expand the world of Click. Particular thanks go to our editor, Mary, whose enthusiasm and helpful guidance have been invaluable while exploring the lives of these vibrant besties.

We'd also like to thank our agent, Elizabeth, for always having our backs.

And of course, all the thanks in the universe to our stellar creative team: designers Andy and Stephanie, letterer Lor, colorist Damali, and absolute superstar/illustrator Kristina. Your hard work and creativity have made *Besties* into the sparkling, sleepover-filled, dance party–infused celebration of friendship we dreamed of.

Lastly, we would like to thank our family and friends for their constant support. Kayla would like to thank Mom, Dad, Grandpa, K, William, and Tyler. Jeffrey would like to thank Karen and Brad.

—Kayla & Jeffrey

I'd like to thank the amazing team behind *Besties* for all the love, patience, and support they've poured into this book. *Besties* is my published comics debut, so I am honoured to be trusted with this wonderful series. I couldn't be more proud of what we've accomplished, and I hope you all feel the same way too. A huge thank-you to Kayla and Jeffrey for being an incredible duo to work alongside. You've been both an inspiration and the ultimate cheerleaders from the first page to the last brushstroke. Also, a big thank-you to Damali for just being utterly fantastic. Your colours make the world feel so lush and vibrant and take my drawings to a whole new level. I'd also like to send a thank-you to my agent, Britt Siess, for helping me every step of the way and just being a star. Everyone's collective efforts have made this book into something truly special, and I'll treasure it forever.

And finally, I'd like to thank all my wonderful friends and family who inspire me every day, keep me going, and are simply incredible people. Thank you, Mom, Dad, and Bryan, for always believing in me and giving me phở when I needed it most. And lastly, a huge thank-you to my friends, at home, online, and across the globe. Your support and faith in me over the years have carried me from my humble webcomic beginnings to my first book on the shelf. So gosh, thank you for believing in this little worm after all these years!

—Kristina

GRAPHIC NOVELS
FOR EVERY READER!